For James J. Casolo, Jr., 1963–1994

—B. G.

The drawings are for me Mum

—P. D.

Rabbit Ears Books is an imprint of Rabbit Ears Productions, Inc.
Published by Simon & Schuster, Inc.
1230 Avenue of the Americas
New York, New York 10020

Manufactured in the United States of America.
2 4 6 8 10 9 7 5 3 1

Library of Congress Cataloging-in-Publication Data
Gleeson, Brian.
Finn McCoul / adapted by Brian Gleeson ; illustrated by Peter de Sève.
p.   cm.
Summary: Retells the Irish folktale in which the giant Finn McCoul and
his very clever wife defeat the brutish giant Cucullin.
ISBN 0-689-80201-3
1. Finn MacCumhaill, 3rd century—Juvenile literature. [1. Finn MacCool.
2. Folklore—Ireland.]   I. De Sève, Peter, ill. II. Title.
PZ8.1.G4594Fi 1995
398.21—dc20   [E] 92-36652

FINN McCOUL

Written by **Brian Gleeson**

Illustrated by **Peter de Sève**

RABBIT EARS BOOKS

IFinn McCoul was the most famous
champion Ireland ever knew. Finn was a giant,
to be sure, but when he was born he was
no bigger than a fire-breathing
dragon, and as giants went
in those days that was a
mite on the wee side.

Now King Coul was Finn's father, and being a
famous Irish giant himself, he took the lad's
small size to heart. "I have a boil on me flank
that's bigger than he is!" said King Coul on
seeing the boy for the first time.

King Coul was so distraught over Finn's size
that he took the child to the castle
parapet, wiped the potato-sized tears
from his eyes, and gently punted him
into the loch below.

Now the grandmother of the lad, King Coul's mother, just happened to be on the shore watching as the infant plunged into the water.

"Why, that's me own flesh and blood splashing about there!" she said, and immediately dove in. In two shakes of a lamb's tail she dragged the child out of the loch and rushed away with him deep into the woods. Finding a nice, stout tree, the grand dame took out her hatchet and chopped a chamber within it. And there the two of them lived.

For years the old woman lovingly fed Finn a diet of tree bark, peat, and the occasional grub. But the child thrived nonetheless. After some time the boy rather outgrew his surroundings, and it was then that his grandmother knew it was time to send him out into the wild and cruel world.

Now such an inauspicious beginning to a life has been known to spoil a man's disposition entirely. But not young Finn! He thanked his grandmother for looking after him, kissed her gently upon the head, and set out to distinguish himself as a great hero.

Why, he was as strong as two dozen oxen, and as swift as forty-three hares. And he trekked all over the emerald countryside, taking a glen at a step, a hill at a leap, and lochs at a bound.

Before too long, Finn took a wife for himself, and her name was Oonagh. Oonagh was a beauty, as they say, and a giantess herself. Aye, and that sun-kissed lass was a clever one, too. They were a matched pair, they were, with Finn's brawn and Oonagh's brain.

Together they lived quite happily upon the top of Knockmany Hill in Ulster. People always wondered why it was that Finn had selected such a windy spot for his dwelling. Now, Finn made his share of excuses for choosing to live in the middle of nowhere, but the real reason Finn made his home atop Knockmany was to see Cucullin coming.

Ah, Cucullin! It sends shivers down my spine to even utter the name. *Cucullin!* No other giant in all of Eire could stand before him. It was said—and I personally know for a fact it is true—that by a single blow of his fist he once flattened a thunderbolt into the shape of a pancake. He always carried it about with him in his pocket. And before he got into a fight with one of his foes, Cucullin would always show them the pancake just to give them a notion of the kind of pulping they were about to receive.

Cucullin had given every giant in Eire a considerable tarring—everyone, of course, but Finn himself. But that was only owing to the fact that whenever Cucullin went after Finn, our hero would run in the opposite direction.

Now at this time Finn was building the causeway from Ireland to Scotland. It was a grand undertaking—even for Finn—so he had his band of champions, called the Fenians, assisting him.

One day down at the causeway, Finn and his men were rearranging the coast and moving a few small cliffs, when he began gnawing upon his thumb. You see, this is how Finn called upon his singular gift for prophecy. Whenever he got into a fix and he couldn't fathom the choices that life so often presents, he would suck his thumb for inspiration and a most curious thing would occur: He would see the future before him as clear as day. For it was in his thumb that his power for prophecy resided. Now, at that precise moment, Finn had divined from his thumb that Cucullin was coming to the causeway to do battle with him. And it was just then that Finn discovered a very warm and sudden fit of affection for his wife.

"I need to see me lovin' Oonagh," said Finn. "Me thumb tells me so. Methinks she's in danger."

"But Finn," pleaded Conan the Bald, one of the Fenians, "what about the causeway?"

Alas, it was no use. Finn was already well on his way to Knock-many.

"God save all here!" said Finn, strutting into his home.

"Musha, Finn," said his wife. "Welcome home to your own Oonagh, ye darlin' bully. And what brought you home so soon, Finn?"

"Why, me sweet rose, nothin' but the purest of love and affection for ye, of course." After Finn spoke, he clapped his thumb into his mouth.

"Finn, sweetness," said Oonagh. "Please don't do that while you're talking to me. It's not polite."

"He's a-comin'," said Finn. "I see him below Dungannon."

"Who's comin'?" said Oonagh. "Who are ye talking about?"

"It's that nasty Cucullin, it is. Oohhh! It's said that when he gets angry and begins to stamp, a dozen earthquakes erupt. And when he does battle with thunderbolts, he flattens them into tiny pancakes and then eats them with honey! A whole hive of it! And with the bees still buzzin' inside it!"

"Gracious, the brute!" said Oonagh.

"I don't know how I'll manage," said Finn. "If I run away again, I'll be disgraced before my people. And me thumb tells me that I must meet him sooner or later."

"Well, my bully, don't be downcast," said Oonagh. "Leave it to me and I'll bring you out of this scrape better than you might on your own."

Now it so happened that Oonagh had a sister named Granua, who lived upon a hill called Cullamore just opposite Knockmany. The beautiful valley that separated the two sisters was only four miles wide, and so on a summer's evening when they wanted to talk, Oonagh and Granua only had to put their heads out the windows of their homes.

"Granua, are you home?" asked Oonagh.

"I am, sister, dear," said Granua. "And how have ye been today?"

"Well, not so well, I'm afraid," said Oonagh. "Would you do us the favor of looking about from your window and telling us what ye see?"

"Why, nothin', sister, dear. 'Tis only a mountain coming over this way," said Granua. "Nothing to trouble yourselves over."

"A mountain! That's no mountain!" said Oonagh. "That's the giant Cucullin and he's coming to leather our Finn. Perhaps if you delay the brute, it will give me a moment to think. Why don't you ask him up for a bite?"

"I only have fifty pounds of butter, and it's not nearly enough to make a cake for that giant," said Granua. "If you toss me over a ton or two, you'll oblige me very much."

So Oonagh got the largest tub of butter she had and called up to her sister.

"Granua, are you ready?" said Oonagh. "I'm going to throw now."

Oonagh gave the butter a mighty heave, but in her anxiety over Cucullin she forgot to say the magic words that were to make it fly to Granua. And so the butter landed with a thud halfway between the two hills.

"My curse upon you, baleful butter," cried Oonagh. "You've disgraced me." And with that said, the butter turned instantly to stone. It lies there today exactly as it came out of Oonagh's hand, with the mark of her four fingers and thumb imprinted upon it.

"Oh, never mind," said Granua. "I will do the best I can to stall Cucullin."

So Granua baked her cake anyway and signaled Cucullin to come up to Cullamore. She placed the cake before the giant, and without so much as a "Thank ye, Miss," Cucullin threw it into his mouth and devoured it in one frightening bite.

"Needs butter," he grunted, licking the last crumbs from his fingers, and proceeded on his way.

In the meantime, Finn was in quite a panic on Knockmany. "Oonagh, can you do nothing for me, woman? Where is all your invention? Will I be skivered like a rabbit before your eyes and have me name disgraced forever before all of Ireland? How can I fight a man who scares the fire out of thunderbolts?"

"There now, be easy, Finn," replied Oonagh. "I've got an idea. Just leave it to me." With that, Oonagh went to work. First she rummaged about and found twenty-one iron griddles. Then she took the griddles and kneaded them into the middle of six loaves of bread. She then baked the loaves on the fire, setting them aside in the cupboard when they were done. Finally, Oonagh took a large pot of new milk, which she made into curds and whey, and then whispered something into Finn's ear. And just as Cucullin was coming across the valley, Oonagh fetched a baby's cradle and instructed Finn to lie down in it.

"Say nothing and follow my lead."

"I will, but I don't like it one bit." Just as he was getting settled, Cucullin burst through the door.

"Be this the home of the great Finn McCoul?" he asked.

"Aye, 'tis indeed," said Oonagh. "But he's not in at the moment. Someone told him that a big basthoon of a giant called Cucullin was down at the causeway looking for him, so he rushed away to catch him. Can I help ye?"

"I am Cucullin," said he, looking puzzled. "And I've been after your husband for twelve months."

Oonagh let out a loud, mocking laugh, and looked at him as if he was only a little pip of a man. "If ye take my advice, ye poor-looking creature, ye'll pray day and night that ye may never see him," said Oonagh. "It will be a black day for you if ye do."

"*Harumpf!*" snorted Cucullin, dismissing Oonagh's warning.

"Ah, now the wind's blowing against the door," said Oonagh. "Seeing as how Finn is away from home, would you be civil enough to turn the house around?"

Now this request took Cucullin aback, for even he didn't do this sort of task on a daily basis. Nevertheless, he pulled the little finger of his right hand three times and went outside. He then put his massive arms about the house and with some effort turned it in a position favorable to the wind.

"Thank ye kindly," said Oonagh. "Please stay and have a bit of me humble fare. Even though you and Finn are enemies, he would scorn me if I didn't treat ye kindly in his own home."

Oonagh brought Cucullin to the table and placed before him the half-dozen loaves of bread she had baked, together with ten sides of bacon and a stack of steaming cabbage.

Cucullin greedily stuffed one of the loaves into his mouth and took a tremendous bite. When Cucullin's teeth struck the griddle that lay in the middle of the loaf, the entire house shook!

"*Arrrggghhh!* Blood and fury!" shouted Cucullin. "And just what sort of bread is this you've given me, I might ask?"

"What's the matter?" said Oonagh.

"Matter!" shouted Cucullin. "Why, what's the matter indeed! Here are the two best teeth in me head smashed to smithereens!"

"Oh, it's a pity that I forgot to tell you that nobody but Finn himself can eat it—and his little mite who sleeps in the cradle over there."

"Take your bread away or I'll not have another tooth in my head!"

"Now, now," said Oonagh. "Don't be waking the child with all your bellyachin'."

Then Finn gave a shriek that startled the giant. *"Goooooo!"*

"Now you've gone and done it. You've awakened him," said Oonagh.

"Ma," said he, "I'm hungry and I want something to eat." Oonagh went to the cradle and gave Finn one of the loaves of bread that had no griddle in it. After a few bites, he realized it was safe, and made the rest of the loaf disappear in two bites.

Cucullin was thunderstruck, and by the look on his face, Oonagh knew her plan was working.

"I'd like to have a look at the lad in the cradle," said Cucullin. "Any child who can manage that bread is in good fighting trim."

"Get up and say hello to our guest, me lamb," said Oonagh, motioning to Finn. "He's terribly shy when company comes. Not many travelers get up our way, ye know."

Finn crawled out of the cradle and toddled over to Cucullin.

"Are you strong as me da?"

"What a boomin' voice in such a young babe!"

"Just a touch of the whoopin' cough," Oonagh explained with a smile.

Then Finn grabbed a white stone and handed it to Cucullin. "Can ye squeeze water out of this white stone?" said Finn.

Now Cucullin was puzzled, but as he intended to humor the lad, he took the stone and squeezed it as hard as he could. But it was no use. He might be able to turn the house around or flatten a thunderbolt into a pancake, but squeezing water out of a rock was something else entirely.

"You call yourself a giant? Me da can do it and he has shown me how. Give me that stone." Finn took the stone from Cucullin and then slyly exchanged it with the curds, just as Oonagh had instructed. And he then squeezed the curds until the whey squirted out in a little shower from his hand, clear as water. "I don't care to waste my time with a giant the likes of you. You had better be out of here before me da comes back, or else he'll make porridge of you—and serve you for dinner!"

Now Cucullin was taken quite aback.

"He is a lucky man, to be sure, to have such a handsome wife and a son who snacks on iron and squeezes water from dry stones. I see I have misjudged him terribly. If it's all the same to ye, I think I'll stay a bit and wait for Finn's return. It would do me proud to make the acquaintance of a great hero such as he. And I shall have to apologize for chasing him hither and yonder for all these months. Yes, apologize I must, even if it takes Finn a fortnight to return."

With that, Cucullin sat next to Finn's cradle and rocked it, somewhat roughly as giants will do, and hummed a soothing, giant lullaby.

Poor Finn saw his very life pass before his eyes. "Ooohhh, me bones."

"What is wrong with the child?" asked Cucullin.

"Um . . . er . . . The poor lad is teething," said Oonagh. "His gums have been smarting lately. There's nothing that can be done."

"I am not so sure of that," said Cucullin. "Me own dear mother had a little trick she used when me choppers come up." With that, Cucullin reached for the flask of spirits he kept in his hip pocket. He poured a touch upon the little finger of his right hand and opened Finn's mouth with his left. Then he massaged Finn's gums with the spirit-soaked finger. "The spirits will dull the boy's pain," said he.

Now it was bad enough to have Cucullin in one's house, but to sit back and take his little finger in the mouth was unpardonable.

"Now just a little bit more, laddie," said Cucullin, as he lovingly administered another dose. "You know, Mrs. McCoul, I think after I've made your husband's acquaintance, I will take a wife so that I may have a son just like yours."

"It's the teeth way in the back of his mouth that are the worst," said Oonagh. "You are such a help, kind man."

And at that moment Oonagh decided to take matters into her own hands. She grabbed the pot that hung in the hearth and rearing back, she hurled it at the head of the giant with all her might. Instead of Cucullin, however, the pot struck poor Finn dead upon the crown. The concussion was so great that Finn clamped down upon Cucullin's little finger, which was still applying the spirits, lopping it off at the third knuckle.

"Arrrgggbhh! Look what the boy has done to me," Cucullin groaned, holding his maimed right hand. "I'm finished!"

You see, the giant's huge strength all lay in the very little finger of his right hand, which Finn had accidentally separated from its master.

Cucullin then let loose with another ear-shattering scream, and then right before the eyes of Finn and Oonagh, he shrunk from the size of a giant to that of a timid little church mouse.

Now Oonagh and Finn had a large tomcat who liked to sleep behind the stove. But all the commotion woke him, and when he came out to investigate, there stood the oddest looking mouse he had ever seen! Without much ado, the tomcat chased the screaming, former giant down Knockmany, around the lochs and across the fields, right into the sea.

"Glory be!" said Finn in triumph. "There isn't a giant in all of Eire as great as meself. I have defeated the great Cucullin!"

Oonagh then picked up her newly dented pot and gazed meaningfully into her dear husband's eyes.

"Er . . . uh . . . or perhaps should I say *we* have defeated the great Cucullin."

And truer words were never spoken.